I0531348

QUACKS

& OTHER STORIES

Subtitled

"penitence.com
and
fenced@nine.com"

Sub-editor

Anne A Gramm

Geoffrey Higges

ISBN: 978-0-6453241-4-3

DEDICATION

To the honest politicians, police, tradespeople, sales personnel and honest medical people who may get tarred with the same bad brush

CONTENTS

QUACKS & OTHER STORIES

ACKNOWLEDGMENTS

To my wife Carole-Anne Fooks for suggestions and
proofreading

QUACKS & OTHER STORIES

1 DOCTORING THE EVIDENCE

In 1950 I got my first motorbike, a BSA Bantam, and in 1954 I got my first car, a 1948 Morris 8. I soon learnt the requirement for constant attention while driving, when leaning back for something on the back seat I ended up in a ditch on the side of the road.

Later in 1957 in a 1937 Ford 8 I had my first brush with the police. I was driving from my lodgings in Cambridge Street in Bristol along the A38 to work at Bristol Aero Engines in Filton when a car came out from a side street in front of me. I braked as much as I could but still just caught the back of the offending car. There did not seem to be much damage to either car, so I went on my way and thought that was the end of the matter.

Two months later I received a summons to appear in court on a charge of dangerous driving. I was surprised and angry because I thought nothing serious had happened and that I was in the right anyway; but not being experienced in such matters I didn't know what to do about it and so four weeks later I ended up in court.

I realized that my case must have been one of many because the court was full of people and police. Eventually the magistrate asked one of the policemen to state the case

For many years the British public were universally described as law-abiding, and the British Police as helpful and honest and without guns.

But since the 1950s, crime has increased, and there has been a succession of inquiries into police activities which has shown that all was not that perfect after all. At the same time these events may have been the catalyst for many researchers to look back and find a complete history of corrupt policing in Britain from its inception in 1829.

for the prosecution. As the policeman proceeded with his statement of how I had been speeding and driving so recklessly as to cause the accident, I think the magistrate must have noticed my open-mouthed amazement at the fabricated story.

When the policemen had finished his statement, the magistrate turned to me and asked for my statement. I said I was not speeding, and that I thought it was the other driver's fault for not pausing before entering the main road.

The magistrate nodded wisely, and looking straight at the two policemen who seemed to have brought my case, said "Now gentlemen, tell me what actually happened in this case!"

The second policeman stood up and without notes said, "It was probably more like Mr. Higges described."

"I thought so" the magistrate said and turning to me again said "I am charging you with Careless Driving and fining you 20 pounds. Please take more care when driving, recognizing that other people can do silly things!"

I left court in somewhat of a daze, not because of the fine I had received, but the way the magistrate had spoken to the police which at the time was so enlightening for one who had grown up believing the British police to be beyond reproach. I have never forgotten that experience.

I could not see the point of why the police would bother to fabricate the evidence in such a minor case. Were the number of convictions they were credited with valued by the extent of the fine, or by the number of years in jail? Or was it just habit?

In the media there are regular stories of police tampering with the evidence or similar. A few days ago, in an Australian city the police had claimed that a transgender woman had been physically violent with them, so they had tasered her and then arrested her. However later in court, CCTV footage showed that it was the police who had attacked the woman for no apparent reason, bashed her and tasered her, then chased after her again to arrest her and concoct their story.

2 DOCTORING CARS

According to the business consultants Hubspot, only 1% of the population trust car salesman. I don't think that statistic applies to car tradesmen, nevertheless for at least the first 40 years of owning cars, nearly every time I took my car in for service it came back with a new problem. This happened in England for the 4 years that I owned cars there, and for the first 40 or 50 years of my life in Australia.

I can no longer remember the specific service places where many "small" faults were deliberately inserted, although I remember many of the tricks used; like interfering with spark plugs, ignition, battery connections, distributor, rotor arm, radiator hose, etc.

Although I could have serviced and fixed many problems myself, I did not like getting my hands dirty, so I would take my car to a garage, where they obviously thought I must be a naïve driver.

In many cases after servicing of my car I would find the "new fault" and it was often a simple case of fixing it myself. Occasionally I would take the car back to the service station and let them fix it, even when I knew what the problem was.

I can describe two cases in detail, because in the first case

It is not difficult to find comments from unhappy customers on the internet, this one in Adelaide (summarised for copyright reasons): "My car was in perfect running order when I took it in for service, but when I got it back it would not run properly. What can I do?"

The answer given showed that there are several options of complaining and suing possible, but all would be both expensive and unlikely to succeed.

I did not know what the new problem was, while the second case was of a different type, but quite hilarious, providing me with a good story to tell many times later. And it involved the same car both times.

In 1970 in South Australia I had a blue Holden Monaro automatic. The car was operating perfectly when I took it in for a regular service to a garage at the north-eastern edge of the city of Adelaide. I collected the car after work just before the garage closed. I did not get very far before there was a succession of hesitant noisy clunks. After stopping, then starting again, the same thing happened. I did a U-turn and headed in violent jerks back to the garage where I parked inside the maintenance area just as they were closing (rather than the outside car park) so I would be sure of getting attention.

Because they were scrambling to shut shop and go home it was not long before a mechanic came up to me and explained I would have to come back in the morning. I said "No, I am staying here until my car is fixed." Obviously getting angry he said, "Wait here, then." Well I did wait, and although it seemed like a long while at the time, it was probably only 3 or 4 minutes before another older mechanic sidled up to me with a half-smile on his face "What's wrong?" he asked.

I started to explain my predicament while he walked slowly over to the left side of my car by the front door, bent down and reached under the car, seemed to fiddle with something, then stood up, still half smiling.

"It's an old trick" he said. "I've just reconnected the vacuum hose to your automatic system. It'll be OK now."
My eyebrows raised with disbelief, but he was off and out of the doors, and I had to drive out before they could close.

I am still not sure what that device was. It could have been a positive crankcase ventilation hose, although I would not have thought that its disconnection would cause the immediate problems I had.

Then there are the disasters which could generously be seen as not deliberate but "accidental quackery".

In 1966 in Adelaide my Triumph Herald refused to start. I suspected it was the battery and called the RAA for help. The RAA man tested the battery, found it was fine, and said "It must be the starter; they often get stuck on this car." Thereupon he went to his van, got out a hammer, and gave the starter 6 healthy blows until it split.

"Aw well, it's definitely broken now" he calmly stated, and quickly drove away.

Again, based on the advice of the RAA man, my wife was advised that the clanking noise she was hearing was not serious, and she could safely drive the 6 kilometres home. She drove home, but by then the engine was ruined with a broken crankshaft.

RAA again. Traditional radiators often boiled and lost water in the hot Australian summers. The safest action was to switch off and wait hours until the engine cooled; however if the radiator needed topping up straight away, the only safe procedure was to slowly take off the cap to gradually reduce the pressure while the engine was idling, thus maintaining a water circulation.

The RAA was called to make sure the topping up was carried out safely. He immediately started to take off the boiling hot radiator cap.

"WAIT! WAIT! I need to start the engine before you do that!"

The RAA man took no notice; the steam blew up in a great shower; and the engine block cracked from the shock.

Another time my wife drove away from a car service with no coolant in the radiator, seizing the engine; and yet another time driving away from a service I investigated scary rattling under the bonnet to find 2 tools left in the engine compartment.

3 SALESMEN

When I was thinking of selling the Monaro, I drove to a well-known car sales yard in the district of Port Adelaide. After starting to look around the yard I was soon approached by a salesman.

"What kind of car do you want?"

"Something not quite so sporty?" I replied.

"We have the very thing!" he said. "Why not take this one for a drive?"

I did have a test drive, and when I returned the salesman was already talking about a trade-in value for my car, saying "I am afraid you will not get very much for your Monaro because of all the rust!"

"I can't see any rust!" I exclaimed.

"Ah, no, but it's underneath all the wearing paint, and it will need a fortune to correct before we can sell it."

This discussion continued, quickly becoming a noisy argument.

Alerted by the noise, a second salesman came across and said, "What is this all about?" I immediately responded annoyingly "It's about the rust on this car!"

"What rust!" he exclaimed, "there is no rust! This car is clearly in perfect condition!"

Various motor scams including on-line scams are described on the website of the Victorian Consumer Affairs https://www.consumer.vic.gov.au/:

1. A former licensed motor car trader has been convicted and fined for odometer tampering and other offences likely to deceive customers.

The trader pleaded guilty to charges under the Motor Car Traders Act 1986 related to changing the mileage readings on two cars, misrepresenting odometer readings to customers on eight cars and recording 14 false readings in its dealings book. The offences were committed between 2018 and 2019.

2. "A professional sounding scammer may call you directly or on-line.

The scammer offers to fix the problem for a fee which when paid you are directed to a website to click on a link that gives them access to your computer. They can steal private information such as bank details, usernames and passwords. You are very lucky if they solve your original problem as well.

The first salesman turned red and took the second man away, obviously explaining to him that I was not buying the car but trading it in!

I did not do business at this car yard, not then, or later.

Salespeople in general are rated as three times more trustworthy than car salesmen in particular; that is 3 x 1% = 3% of the population trust salespeople in general.

That does not mean of course that you will only get satisfaction three times out of a hundred when buying something. Although you might begin to think so if you had gone through our recent experience dealing with a supposedly reputable company. In fact it was hard to distinguish between the salespeople, the tradesmen, and the company itself.

To summarise an extremely long and harrowing story, we paid in full for a particular expensive house item.

It was over 2 months of incompetence before we received it.

It was a further 9 months of incompetence after the installation before they managed to get it to operate properly.

"Remember, the secret to selling is 'sincerity' ... once you can fake that you've got it made."

Courtesy salesman.org

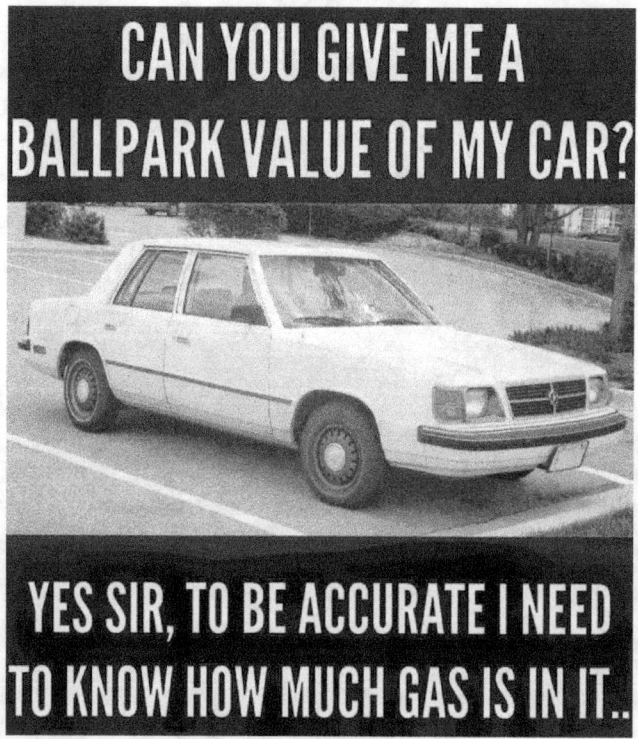

Courtesy fetchaquote.com

4 DOCTORING EQUIPMENT

My experience with some equipment repairers is similar to the car situation. Yes, they are often able to fix the fault you took it in for, but they are also able to cleverly adjust some item to cause trouble so that sooner or later you have to call back.

In one case I had a new computer made up especially for video editing (I still have it). I had a lot of trouble getting it to start; often it would not start at all. Three times I took it back, to no avail.

The fourth time I took it back, there was a different person on the desk. After I described the particular problem, he switched on my computer, cutting short the starting procedure to go to the System page, and typed in a different value for one item.

I had no more starting problems.

It seems that my computer failed to start when external hard drives were attached, and a direction in the System page needed to be set to C drive, to stop the computer searching all the attachments, and sometimes failing to start at all.

Was the simple incorrect setting deliberate? I don't know.

I had a different kind of problem with a video camera. I took my camera in for repair. I had to pay $60 up front.

After 6 weeks I asked for a progress report – still being repaired. At 4-week intervals thereafter I asked for my camera back – still being repaired.

After 6 months I told them I wanted my camera back regardless, otherwise I would report them to Consumer Affairs. I got my camera back – repaired.

After a number of enquiries I discovered that the most likely cause for the delay was that members of the staff were using my camera.

5 BAD DESIGN

Bathroom Shower design.

You can buy the equipment needed for a shower in your bathroom, but a licenced plumber is need for the piping while a licenced builder would normally complete the installation.

My particular requirements would be for a walk-in shower with plenty of room for entry and internally e.g. 800mm x 800mm, non-slip floor, no wall fixings below waist level, and a safety handrail on the wall above waist level. A non-slip floor is preferred for the whole bathroom as well.

Australia does have recommended standards for showers, but unfortunately they are not mandatory.

After a game of golf in 2003 I slipped and fell in the showers in the clubroom. It might not have been too serious, and it might not have happened at all, if the club's shower design had taken notice of Australian Standard guidelines for public showers.

Unfortunately the shower I was in had a projecting ceramic footrest about 200mm above floor level.

My back landed right on top of the footrest resulting in a lot of pain, a massive black bruise covering my whole back, several broken ribs and a collapsed lung.

I ended up in intensive care, requiring days of blood draining from my left lung resulting in more than 20% permanent loss of capacity in my left lung.

As the pain in my back and chest subsided over the five-month recovery period, I became aware that my right foot had been injured also, but with no apparently serious symptoms other than mild pain and feeling weak and unstable.

"Careful in the bathroom—we just had it reimagined."

Courtesy Joe Dator/The New Yorker

6 FAKE DOCTORS

In 1973 in Plympton near Adelaide, after several months discomfort, I was diagnosed by my local doctor with right inguinal hernia. An appointment was made for surgery at a hospital near Hutt Street in Adelaide.

After settling in my bed with several others in the hospital ward I was surprised to find that the operating surgeon was my local doctor. Nevertheless the operation took place seemingly without problems and I was returned to my bed.

Two days later I was feeling quite well so I got up gingerly and went to the toilet. I was returning to my bed and was managing reasonably well when I was suddenly accosted by a nurse almost screaming "What are you doing out of bed!"

Soon after she had shoved me back in bed, the doctor/surgeon came hurrying in and ordered me sternly that I must not move for 2 weeks. (Of course nowadays the same operation is day surgery, patients returning home 2 hours after the operation.)

That turned out to be a very boring 2 weeks, apart from a couple of interesting incidents. However the worst outcome of not getting appropriate exercise for so long was that it took years to heal properly, often with intervening pain.

An ABC News report posted by Philippa Martyr 10 Apr 2018 showed just how easy it is to pretend to be a medical specialist, mainly because doctors as a whole are trusted people. Also colleagues assume someone else must have checked their credentials, even when faulty practices are evident; and there is the ever-present danger of being a whistle-blower. In regional areas the difficulty of hiring staff may tempt a more cursory check of the paperwork.

While still in hospital I was chatting to a newly arrived neighbour in the next bed. He said he had a hernia too, but he was managing that satisfactorily with a brace. He said he was having more pain with his appendix. So he had actually entered hospital for an appendectomy.

He had his operation that evening; then suddenly in the early hours of next morning I was wakened by some swearing in the next bed.

"What is the matter?" I asked drearily.

Splutter, splutter, "I've had the wrong operation! He's done my hernia instead of my appendix!"

Two days later the peace was disturbed again, in the middle of the day this time. A man came rushing into the ward shouting "Where's that doctor! Where's that doctor!" He was holding up one arm waving it about. A nurse came in trying to calm him down, telling him the doctor wasn't in the hospital.

He was yelling "Look what he's done to my hand – I'm

going to sue him! Look what he's done to my hand!"

He was waving his hand around so much that I had difficulty seeing it properly. But then he started going round the ward showing it to everybody and I could see that apparently he could not open up his fingers properly. I eventually managed to get the picture that our doctor had operated on his hand for arthritis, and the operation had made it ten times worse.

During my two weeks stay at the hospital, I heard several more horror stories about this doctor. So after finally leaving hospital I tried to find out more about him. But I could not find anything about any qualifications or background at all.

Two years later I discovered that the hospital had closed, and the doctor/surgeon had left the country.

For complaints referring to any medical situation, health related or administrative or money related, go to this government health website:
https://www.health.gov.au/health-topics/medicare-compliance/reporting-incorrect-billing-or-claiming-or-suspected-fraud.

This website lists the kind of complaint they deal with directly (such as the several commonwealth health programs), and secondly a list of situations where the complaint or report should be reported to a particular authority (such as those referring to the professional conduct of a health provider, and anything to do with Covid-19.)

---

7 QUACKS ?

In 1949 I was called up for National Service in England. I travelled to Sheffield for my medical where I was told that I was unfit for service in the Army, and that I must choose the Airforce or the Navy. As it happened I chose the RAF.

It was 50 years later that I began to feel the effects of my flat feet as I started having problems with my right foot feeling weak and vulnerable, together with the accident referred to above. (Not to mention the fungus on my nails, and the big toenails growing in all directions.)

I was referred to a so-called Podiatrist, and I told him about my weak right foot. (The condition of my nails was obvious.)

The Podiatrist looked at my feet and said "Interesting!"

He took a sharp needle-like instrument and stuck the sharp end in in my bare left foot. "Ouch!" I muttered.

He took the needle and stuck it in my right foot. I did not respond.

"Could you feel that?" he asked, sticking the needle in my right foot again.

> *The first website I came to when looking up the qualifications of Podiatrists was called LetsRun with the address https://www.letsrun.com/forum/flat_read.php?thread=355 4819.*
>
> *The heading of the front-page article was "Are Podiatrists quacks like Chiropractors".*
>
> *Comments in the article included "Podiatrists are not quacks but are very limited in what they can do."*
>
> *"I should have gone to an Orthopaedic surgeon."*
>
> *"Chiros are more likely to be quacks but can also be excellent at treating soft tissue injuries. The real problem with Chiros is that insurance companies pay them a fraction of what doctors get. So, Chiros will want to see you three times a month for the rest of your life."*
>
> By the way my own experience with chiropractors is being left in a room on my own with a machine while the chiropractor circulates among several other patients in the facility. Profitable for the owner perhaps, but no help to me.

Surprised, I said "No, I did not feel anything."

"Interesting" he said.

"I will get a pair of orthotics for you. We will take the shape of your foot with plaster, and I will call you when they are ready. Just $450 – on top of my fee."

And so for the next 3 years my walking was slightly eased, but my right foot was basically still weak, and of course my nails were discoloured and all over the place, so I obtained a referral to a so-called Foot Specialist.

I told him my story, and without looking at my feet he responded "That should all be better in 2 or 3 years. Thank you for coming, you can pay at the desk." An expensive 5 minutes.

Several years later I was attending a different medical centre which happened to have a resident Podiatrist. Because I was slightly limping by this stage I decided to try for a diagnosis of my foot again.

I told the Podiatrist the story of my right foot and she said "I can sell you a better pair of inserts than the ones you have, for just $650. Just walk up and down the passage outside while I take some photographs of you walking. Then I will phone you when the orthotics are ready."

6 months later I was standing more or less still and upright at home when my right foot exploded. That is the only word I can use to describe the sensation of all the ligaments and bones in my foot coming apart very painfully and making it impossible for me to take any weight on the foot.

My wife helped me bind my foot to give some feeling of stability, and amazingly after about 2 weeks my foot was starting to pull itself together again, so that now I am walking short distances again, with carefully chosen firm supporting shoes, but without orthotics.

Immediately after this foot episode I had obtained a referral to a (different) foot specialist. After 5 minutes of consultation with this specialist, no conclusion was reached and no actions or treatment recommended. He just said, "Let me know if it happens again!"

So I still have a weak right foot of about half strength, and funny toenails; but thankfully walking sufficiently well to play 9 holes of golf each week (although with 60% lung effectiveness and 60% blood flow to my left leg).

9 BUREAUCRACY

I know everyone has stories about government bureaucracies, and banks and big organisations in general, where everything that goes wrong is someone else's fault and no one is ever responsible. There is a particular government department in Australia which is universally known for such notoriety, and we have had a few experiences of its failings ourselves. The following story would fill a whole book if told in detail, yet for the most part it would not be original or unique because so many others have had similar experiences.

In this instance we were making a claim for welfare assistance in a particular area. In typical bureaucratic fashion it was claimed that there was one simple form to be completed which could take up to an hour. Days later we had completed 6 required forms and filled in nearly 100 pages.

Since that time we have discovered that this always occurs with "simple" government forms because every other question you come to refers you to yet another form which has to be completed. On top of all this, everything has to be verified by statements from all the people, banks, institutions etc., who are mentioned in all the forms you end up with, adding further to the time, the paperwork and the stress.

This is an extract from an article by Anna Yeatman, The Guardian 15 September 2019. "Public Bureaucracy and Customer Service: The Case of Centrelink 1996– 2004"

In 1996 the newly elected conservative Australian government led by Prime Minister John Howard took as one of its first initiatives the establishment of a one-stop shop for the provision of government services. While the largest component of these services was to be 'the administration of entitlements under social security legislation', the new agency was to 'deliver services for a number of portfolios and integrate these into a common point of customer contact'.

Carers of teenagers with disabilities say their Centrelink payments are being cut off and that some parents are going without support for months while paperwork is assessed. [This is because] The federal government requires people who are receiving the carer allowances to transfer it to an adult payment when their child turns sixteen.

Carers have to submit forms that prove their child's identity and place of residence, detail their caring routine and their child's cognitive function and behaviour and submit a new medical report from the child's treating health professional.

So when our turn comes in the queue, we thankfully hand in our bundle of forms and are told it will be about 6 weeks before we will be contacted to inform us of the outcome.

Two months later we had not heard anything.

After a further week or two, we still had not heard anything, so we joined the queue in the service centre again, and when it was our turn we asked for information about our application.

The attendant went away, eventually came back and said, "There is no application here from you, nor in the whole commonwealth records."

In the Guardian 15 September 2019:

1. Six people recount their interactions with Centrelink and the government's welfare programs, which range from absurd to frustrating to insulting. Earlier this year a scathing Senate report said the Jobactive scheme – the government's employment service – had unleashed a "bureaucratic nightmare" on jobseekers.

2. The Robodebt scheme saw 443,000 Australians wrongly pursued by Centrelink for $1.7 billion in welfare debts they didn't owe, creating a lot of distress to many people. So Centrelink is now chasing about 20,000 Australians who are owed money or will have their debts cancelled through the controversial welfare recovery scheme.

I have listed above just three examples of what could be termed problems with "corporate or federal bureaucracy" affecting individual's lives, but there are countless examples of ongoing frustrations of "local bureaucracy" similar to our own experience.

You can imagine our open mouths and rather tense altercations that followed. We gave a detailed description of the person we gave our forms to, and we asked to see the manager.

The answers we received astonished us even further. "There is no such person you describe who has ever worked here – and we do not have a manager!"

This has been the only response we have ever received.

Since that time we have experienced other frustrating times dealing with them on other matters, and we have heard many similar stories about this government organisation.

Courtesy ginamussio.com/

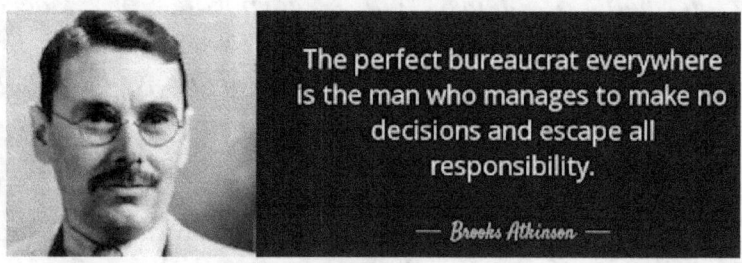

Courtesy azquotes.com

10 UNREAL ESTATE AGENTS

Roy Morgan Poll 1916: Top 10 most untrustworthy Australian professions:

1. Car salesman (voted most untrustworthy for the last 30 years at least)
2. Advertising people
3. Real estate agents, salesmen in general
4. Insurance brokers
5. Union leaders
6. Stockbrokers
7. State MPs
8. Federal MPs
9. TV reporters
10. Newspaper journalists

We all know that advertising is suspect, but how can a Real Estate agent do the dirty on you? The following experience is one way.

A 30-acre farm in the Adelaide Hills in South Australia was advertised in the local paper. I contacted the agent and arranged to be taken by him around the property after I had finished work.

For a change, the actual property turned out to be better

than the advertisement seemed to indicate. Everything was in good order; the house, the sheds, and the land itself.

While he was driving me home we were discussing the property and I ended up confirming to the agent that I would buy the property and pay a deposit. He replied that as his office was closed now, I should come in first thing in the morning to sign all the papers and make payment.

Next morning I did just that, only to be told "Oh sorry, my manager has just bought the property!"

Perhaps you have some other stories justifying the Real Estate Agent's position on the untrustworthy scale.

One way you might lose an investment property you already own is for an overseas entity to first convince an Australian real estate agent that the ownership has changed to them, and secondly that they now wish to sell. The agents get a nice fat commission, and you suddenly stop getting rent. Ref: https://www.reinsw.com.au/.

It is easy to find examples of real estate scams on the internet, many of them however are not by the agents themselves.

[While I was checking the Australian Real Estate website for their comments on fraud, a message appeared in red saying that they were being hacked, and that you should not try to visit their pages on rental properties.]

---

11 TRAVEL AGENTS

Posted by the International Air Travel Association:

Fraud is rapidly increasing in the travel industry and the chance you may land on a fake airline or travel agent website is unfortunately real.

Fraudulent online travel and flight booking agencies operate internationally. These websites can look highly professional, some even displaying the IATA logo to appear legitimate. We do all we can to try and stop fraud, but you have to know that an IATA reference on a travel or cargo website or social media page does not necessarily mean that they are IATA-accredited.

Because this is a growing concern, we suggest using only verified agencies.

Apparently some people do not like using travel agents because they believe it will cost more. Others think a travel agent is more likely to give them a standard package rather than one tailored more closely to their needs.

We have travelled a lot – more than 70 countries visited – and found that it depends mainly on the individual person you get to deal with. To help ensure a stress-free process, we carry out as much research as we can ourselves, on the internet and even with preliminary discussions with a genuine travel agent. Then we write down our requirements for the places we want to visit and what aspects of the visit we want to focus on, together with our desired travel arrangements (flights, accommodations, tours) and give this to the agent.

> *ABC News 31 March 2016*
>
> *Northern Territory Police have confirmed a further 10 travel agencies are being investigated over the potential rorting of a government travel concession scheme.*

We have found it is best to work with an agency whose sole business is travel; not a company whose first interests are elsewhere directed, and just want to cash in on the popularity of travel as a side issue.

We made the latter mistake once, just once. After giving us a quote for a trip, we paid the deposit, and 2 weeks before leaving we paid the full amount - to the female agent who worked for a company that was not foremost a travel agency. One week later we received a call from the agent to come in and pay $1000 more because the prices had gone up.

5 days before we were due to leave we had another call to say prices had gone up again and we must call in and pay another $500 before the agent

> *https://www.news.com.au 29 October 2021*
>
> *A Victorian travel consultant gambled away more than $600,000 in refunds due to go to clients during the height of the coronavirus pandemic after defrauding his/her employer.*

could give us our tickets and other information. We had to go to a different office a long way away this time because we were told our female agent had moved. When we got there we were told our original person was out to lunch; we waited but she never returned and we had to deal with another person.

We had to pay of course to get our tickets because there was so little time left before leaving on holiday.

The Covid-19 lockdowns causing cancellation of holidays have also caused many people to have trouble getting refunds from travel agents at home and abroad, some companies only offering only credit for a limited time.

Then of course there are the fake travel agent scams.

It is one of the most common travel scams out there, along with travel club membership rip-offs. It happens especially when hot destinations are on everybody's mind. Criminals create great looking websites for "new" travel agencies offering amazing deals. You pay your deposit, or even more, and hear no more from them.

According to IATA, approximately 90% of all emails sent worldwide are spam, spoof and phishing attempts.

Payment fraud costs the air transport industry an estimated US $858 million annually, approximately US $639 million of which is borne by airlines and the remainder by other companies in the travel industry.

Courtesy olsenolearytravels.com

Courtesy openjaw.com

12 INTERNET SCAMS

By now most people will have come across attempted scams on the internet, usually via email.

One type of scam entices you into an action which sounds like you can make money, or meet an interesting person, but along the way you have to pay more and more to the scammer to achieve what turns out to be an imaginary outcome.

The second most common scam is an email (or phone call) that purports to come from a reputable organisation like your bank, the post office, the tax department or other government office. They will order you to "click here" to complete a form to confirm or update your personal details. The scammer can then use your information to raid your bank or steal your identity.

A third type of scam is particularly dangerous, particularly if you are earning your living through your computer. The email can look like one of the above, or even more innocent. If you click for any reason - to get more information, or even "to unsubscribe", a virus will be released that will cripple your computer.

In the early days of the internet a "hacker" was someone

who did this for fun. These days the hacker is more likely to follow up with a phone call telling you to pay $500 ($1 million for a big business) before they will clear your computer.

When I recognize a scam (every day) I delete it twice – once out of the inbox to the trash, and then delete it again out of the trash. The following is a typical innocent looking email which you must not click on or reply to:

Hey Friend,

On behalf of the entire team, I want to congratulate you on your success.

After much hard work and patience, you're finally in.

You can check in and confirm your gifts here.

We're about to let you in on the 3k per day - set and forget position that you've been waiting for the past 3 months.

I know it took a while, but this is a first come, first serve position, so your patience is now being rewarded!

So go ahead, watch this video to get started now!

Talk Soon,

Alex E.

In order to unsubscribe from this mailing list, please click here

NOTE: See the appendix for a list of general spams prevalent in Australia today.

13 PLAGIARISM

In 1970 I devised a new method for calculating the strength of various structural elements in torsion (twisting) and wrote a scientific paper explaining the method. I submitted it to an American machine design publication where it was sent to a US professor for the usual peer review.

Some weeks later I received a letter from the magazine rejecting my paper, saying it was not suitable for their magazine.

Some weeks later again my article did appear in the magazine but it was claimed to be written by the professor who had reviewed my paper, my name not being mentioned.

I have invented several games over the years, mainly board games. One such game was a board game based on Australian Rules Football involving 2 players (teams) who could move the ball around the board (playing field) and score goals or behinds – all according to throws of a dice.

I took the full design of the board, men and rules to a local professional patent attorney with a view to it being patented. He said "Yes" he would either be able to patent it or register the design so that it would be protected.

Some weeks later I still had not heard anything from the attorney. When I asked for some explanation he claimed, "It all takes time!".

You may guess what's coming next.

Not many weeks later, after having a coffee in a local shopping mall, I was browsing amongst the monopolies and other games in a small games shop, when I saw it – a professionally produced box and contents of my game!

I did not buy it.

Actually I don't think a lot of other people bought a copy either, because I have never heard of anyone playing it.

14 CONCLUSIONS

Life is full of bad experiences but also good experiences. We need to appreciate and enjoy the good experiences while they last and stay resilient through the bad experiences, and hopefully learn from them.

We cannot go through life expecting everyone we meet to be aiming to cheat us. What a harrowing and miserable life that would be. No, expect everyone we deal with to be genuine at least until proven otherwise. We must approach every relationship and adventure with positive expectation to get the most out of life, while learning how to manage unhappy experiences by coming back to the things and the people that we know and trust.

Remember it is quite often our bad experiences that are the ones that make the best stories to entertain and bore people with, later in life.

Finally, almost every bad experience is almost certainly not unique – it has probably happened to hundreds or even thousands of people previously. These days you can both verify this, and find options on how to proceed, by searching the internet.

Solution to anagrams: "incompetence" and "confidence men"

REFERENCES

"Crooked Cops: a century of bribes, beatings and bungs from the British police" Simon Basketter, 2011
https://socialistworker.co.uk/

"Operation Countryman - The Flawed Enquiry into London Police Corruption" Dick Kirby, 2020

"Line of Duty - The Real Story of British Police Corruption" Wensley Clarkson, 2020

"The shocking truth about police corruption in Britain" Neil Darbyshire, in The Spectator, 7 March 2015

HELP

If you have been the victim of a scam, contact your bank as soon as possible and contact the platform on which you were scammed to inform them of the circumstances.

More information on scams is available on https://www.scamwatch.gov.au/, including how to make a report and where to get help.

If you have experienced a loss online and believe the perpetrator is located in Australia, you can also report the scam to https://www.cyber.gov.au/acsc/report who triage reports and allocates them to the relevant law enforcement authorities for further action.

Victims of identity theft, or cybercrime can contact https://www.idcare.org/, a free government-funded service that will work with you to develop a specific response plan to your situation and provide support. You can also contact idcare on 1800 595 160.

ABOUT THE AUTHOR

Enjoyer of 99.9% good experiences

Writer and user of computer programs since 1970

Website author, qualified proofreader

Book authorships:

- *Search Geoffrey Higges in goodreads.com*

Extensive medical experience, including:

- *30+ different medical episodes*
- *Encounters with physiotherapists, podiatrists and chiropractors*
- *Sufferer of hospital food*
- *Excellent care and treatment from most health professionals*

Owner/maintainer of several early moto-bikes and cars

Qualified mechanical engineer

Concorde passenger

APPENDIX

LIST OF MOST COMMON SCAMS

Make sure you bookmark the Australian Government website *moneysmart.gov.au* where you will find a list of well over one thousand (1,0000) companies which you should not deal with.

The companies on this list:
- have made unsolicited calls and emails about financial services or products
- do not hold a current Australian financial services (AFS) licence or Australian credit licence from ASIC.

The Australian Competition and Consumer Commission (ACCC) also has a website *scamwatch.gov.au* where it lists the most common scams in Australia at the present time:

- Since August 2021, many Australians have been getting scam text messages about missed calls, voicemails or deliveries. The text messages ask you to tap on a link to download or access something. They ask you to download an app to track or organise a time for a delivery, hear a voicemail message, or view photos that have been uploaded. However, the message is fake, and the app is actually malicious software called Flubot. Do not click or tap on the link. Delete the message immediately.

- Phone-based scams accounted for over $63.6 million (31 per cent) of the losses. Scammers call or text people and claim to be from well-known businesses or government to steal people's personal information. "Scammers are pretending to be from companies such as Amazon or eBay and claiming large purchases have been made on the victim's credit card. When they pretend to help you process a refund, they actually gain remote access to your computer and steal your personal and banking details."

Some scammers are falsely identifying themselves as a Federal Agent and telling victims they have identified suspicious activity linked to their bank accounts. They then request personal details, including a Medicare number, address, and bank details. The fake representatives ask their victim to deposit money into an AFP account.

- Investment scams reported to Scamwatch have cost Australians over $70 million in the first half of this year, more than the total losses reported to Scamwatch for all of 2020, and projected losses are set to reach $140 million by the end of the year.

"More than half of the $70 million in losses were to

cryptocurrency, especially through Bitcoin, and cryptocurrency scams were also the most commonly reported type of investment scam, with 2,240 reports." Scammers pretend to have highly profitable trading systems based on individual expertise or through algorithms they developed. Many of these scams also use fake celebrity endorsements to try and enhance their legitimacy.

In general, if you receive an email or text message that is unknown, unsolicited or you suspect to be fraudulent, including messages with a one-time code that you didn't initiate, the advice is:

- Don't reply to the SMS or email
- Don't provide any personal details
- Don't click on any links
- Don't open any attachments
- Don't call any numbers given in the SMS or email
- Don't share any content of the SMS or email with anyone
- Report the email or SMS to **Scamwatch**
- Email **your phone provider** and give a screenshot of the suspected fraud message, the date and time you received it, how many times you received it and your mobile number.

Yet more scams include:

- Social Security number phishing
- Free money offers

- Amazon and package deliveries phishing
- Computer tech support
- Phony relationships
- Debt collection
- Online classified listings
- Extortion emails
- Grandchild imposter
- Bank/financial institution
- Offers to buy your car
- Offers to sell you a car